DATE DUE   AUG 0 5

SEP 29 05			
MAR 23 06			
GAYLORD			PRINTED IN U.S.A.

Little Horse

Little Horse

Betsy Byars

Illustrated by David McPhail

An Early Chapter Book
Henry Holt and Company
New York

Henry Holt and Company, LLC
Publishers since 1866
115 West 18th Street, New York, New York 10011
www.henryholt.com

Library of Congress Cataloging-in-Publication Data
Byars, Betsy Comer.
Little Horse / Betsy Byars; illustrated by David McPhail.
p.   cm.
Summary: Little Horse falls into the stream and is
swept away into a dangerous adventure and a new life.
[1. Horses—Fiction.] I. McPhail, David M., ill. II. Title.
PZ7.B9836 Li 2001   [Fic]—dc21   00-40983

ISBN 0-8050-6413-3 / First Edition—2002 / Designed by Donna Mark
Printed in the United States of America on acid-free paper. ∞

5   7   9   10   8   6   4

Contents

Little Horse

1

The Valley of Little Horses

Little Horse lived in a small valley. No human had ever put foot there. It was not on any map.

A clear stream gave him water. A meadow gave him green grass.

He slept in a cave beside his mother. He played in the fields with the other colts. He raced beside his father.

One day, Little Horse was thirsty. He went to the stream alone.

He leaned over the water.

He saw a horse looking back at him.

Little Horse wanted to play. He leaned closer.

His nose touched the water, and the face of the horse disappeared in the ripples.

He leaned close again.

This time his hooves slipped on the bank.

Little Horse fell into the stream.

The water began to carry Little Horse away from the shore. He swam for the bank.

Finally he reached it, but here the bank was steeper. It was not the gentle slope where the horses drank.

Little Horse's hooves scratched uselessly at the slick rocks. He tried to get a footing again and again. And the water kept carrying him farther from home.

2

A Distant Cry

Little Horse saw there was a bend in the stream ahead. He saw the low rocks. He could climb these.

Little Horse knew this was his chance. His heart beat faster. He swam hard, but the water was swift and fickle. Instead of pushing him toward the rocks, as he had hoped, the swirling current bore him around the bend.

He swam against the current. He struggled with all his might. He knew this was not just his chance. It was his last chance.

But the water held him.

He lifted his head and whinnied. There was fear and longing in his cry.

None of the horses heard him—not even his mother. She was up in the green meadow with the other horses.

But, as if she sensed something was wrong, she lifted her head and neighed. She looked around. She didn't see her colt.

She ran to the small meadow where the colts played. Little Horse was not there.

She ran to the cave. No Little Horse.

She ran to the stream. She could not see Little Horse there either.

Around the bend, Little Horse raised his head above the current. He saw the last of his homeland.

3

Safe, Unsafe

Little Horse struggled bravely in the current. He knew the water was carrying him far, far from his valley. But Little Horse was helpless.

He looked from one side of the stream to the other. He hoped for shallow water so he could wade to safety. He hoped for a miracle.

The stream went around another bend.

The water was even swifter here. He felt something push against his back. He looked around. His eyes were wide with fright.

It was a log.

Little Horse swam in a small circle. He threw his front legs over a limb.

For the moment he was safe. And, he thought, if only the log would drift closer to shore, he could get off.

Then he heard the noise.

It was a noise Little Horse had never heard before. He lifted his head to hear it better.

The noise was like the sound of rain. But the sky above was blue. The noise was like the sound of thunder. But the sky above was blue.

How could this be? Little Horse wondered.

The strange noise was getting louder.

At least I am safe on this log, he thought. And it cannot be a storm because the sky is blue.

The stream rounded another bend. Little Horse's hopes faded. Now he saw what was making the noise—a waterfall. He let go of the log. He swam as hard as he could for the bank.

Little Horse was almost there when the current caught him and swept him over the edge.

4

The Island

Little Horse went under the water. He bobbed up. He went under again. He bobbed up.

This time he found himself beside the log. He held on. He rested his head against the wood as if he'd found a friend.

It was almost dusk when the log and Little Horse touched an island. Little Horse stumbled onto the land.

His legs wobbled, the way they had when he was newly born. He felt as unsure as he had the first time he stood beside his mother. But then his mother had been there. She had licked him dry. Her nose had steadied him. Her breath had warmed him.

He was glad to be on land, but he saw there was no shelter here—only sand. His hooves left tiny prints as he walked from one end of the island to the other.

Still, he would have a chance to rest. He curled up on the highest part of the island. He closed his eyes.

Little Horse did not sleep. He heard a noise that struck fear into his heart—the beating of wings overhead.

The one thing the little horses feared in their valley—their one enemy—came from the sky.

When they heard the beating of wings, when a warning shadow swept the ground, they ran for the cave.

Little Horse remembered that one of the older horses had not been quick enough. He had been grabbed by the dark claws. He got away, but he bore the scars forever.

Little Horse looked up and saw the enemy. It circled above him.

5

Hawk

Little Horse scrambled to his feet. He looked around in desperation. There was no safe place. No cave here. No low bushes to hide beneath.

The dark form in the sky circled closer. Its shadow swept over Little Horse. Little Horse's blood turned cold. He began to run. He glanced over his shoulder.

The bird dove from the sky, directly at Little Horse.

Little Horse remembered how the old horse had dodged this way and that. He did the same thing.

The bird missed on the first pass. Little Horse glanced up. He saw the bird turn and come back for him.

Another dive. This time Little Horse felt the beat of the wings. The claws grazed his side. He ran this way, that way, but the bird only came back again and again.

Little Horse found himself at the end of the island. The bird was making another dive. She gave a cry as if she knew this would be her last.

Little Horse looked this way, that way.

There was no place else for him to run. So Little Horse did the last thing in the world he wanted to do. Little Horse plunged back into the stream.

6

A Forest of Flowers

This time the stream was kind to Little Horse. It sent him away from the island. His hooves touched the far shore.

The bird was still overhead, circling, watching, waiting. Little Horse moved quickly up the bank and into a forest.

There, he crouched motionless. He did not want the enemy to know where he hid.

Those sharp eyes could see any telltale movement of the leaves.

Little Horse waited a long time. He saw that he was in a forest unlike any he had seen before. It was strange and beautiful.

The tops of the trees were yellow and white and blue. Sweet air filled his lungs.

Little Horse realized these were not trees at all. They were flowers. He was in a forest of flowers.

He picked his way through the stems. This was a strange land he had come to— a land where the forests were made of flowers.

Little Horse stopped at the edge of the forest. He peered out, looking to the sky to see if the bird was still there. The sky was empty. Its color was fading fast.

Little Horse stepped out and looked around in amazement. For the first time in his life, Little Horse realized that he was small.

7

The Cave

He stood for a moment without moving. The world he saw seemed to have been made for things bigger than he.

The rocks around him were huge. Their shapes were strange. He touched them with his nose. They were cold.

The trees were even larger. Their branches reached for the sky. They hid the setting sun.

Little Horse realized that night was coming. He had to find shelter. He searched the roots of these huge trees. In one of them he found a place. Some animal had dug a hole there and made a cave. Little Horse looked inside. This animal had made a nest of dry grass.

Little Horse glanced around to see if the animal was in sight. No. And, he thought, surely if the animal was coming, he would already be inside, safe against the night. Little Horse was grateful. He went inside and curled up.

He was scared.

He was cold.

Worst of all, he was alone. For the first time in his life, Little Horse would not sleep beside his mother.

After a while, he stopped shivering. Little Horse slept.

8

Enemy in the Grass

In the morning, Little Horse opened his eyes.

The sun was shining on the water in the stream below, turning it to silver. That was as it had been in his valley.

He stumbled out from his cave in the tree. He lifted his head. Now he could smell something that had also been in his valley. It was grass, and Little Horse was hungry.

He moved around the tree. The roots were big and gnarled. Then, nose in the air, he headed for the meadow.

The grass was tall. Little Horse had to stretch his neck to reach the tender tips. This grass tasted almost as good as that in his valley.

Suddenly there was a rustling in the grass. Little Horse froze.

The rustling came closer . . . closer . . . closer.

Little Horse looked up.

There was no horse with ears like this.

No horse so big.

Little Horse knew at once this was another enemy.

His heart beat wildly. He turned and darted into the thicker grass. The animal did too.

Little Horse ran this way, that way.

The animal did too.

Then the animal put one large paw on Little Horse's back, pinning him to the ground.

Little Horse could run no more.

9

Thunder!

Little Horse threw back his head. He whinnied with fright. His heart beat so wildly that the sound was like thunder. The little horse realized that the sound he heard was not his heart. It was thunder.

The sound came closer. The sound grew louder. The paw was lifted from his back.

Little Horse was startled, but he knew what he had to do. He began to run.

The thunder followed him. The ground beneath him trembled.

This was an enemy more dangerous than water. More dangerous than what came from the sky. More fearsome than the animal that was bigger than a horse. This was an enemy so terrible that the ground itself trembled.

Little Horse found himself back at the tree.

There was the cave. His cave.

He darted inside and waited, his heart pounding.

The sound of thunder followed. It stopped at the tree.

Little Horse crouched against the back of the cave.

And then what Little Horse feared happened. The animal reached into the cave. Little Horse was caught in its grasp.

10

Pocket Horse

Little Horse was lifted out of the cave. He glanced over his shoulder.

This was the biggest animal Little Horse had ever seen. He was bigger than the trees of his valley.

The animal made noises.

Little Horse had never heard such sounds. He threw back his head. He whinnied with fright.

Something stroked his back. The touch was soft, but Little Horse was still afraid.

Little Horse threw back his head. He neighed again and again.

The animal got to his feet. He took Little Horse with him. Little Horse was lifted higher than he had ever been in his life. Now he was too afraid to neigh.

The animal made more strange noises. Then, to his relief, Little Horse felt himself being lowered.

He was put in something soft and warm. It was dark too, like the cave where he had slept beside his mother.

Little Horse curled into the softness. But his body trembled as if he were cold.

The cave began to jiggle in a soothing manner. Little Horse sensed that he was being carried away.

The noise of the water grew fainter, and Little Horse knew he was being carried into the rising sun.

Then he heard sounds that caused his heart to pound with hope—the neigh of a horse, and another. The sound of hooves.

Little Horse struggled to his feet.

11

The Land of Big Horses

Little Horse stood on his hind legs and pawed at the edge of his cave. He wasn't tall enough to reach the top. He neighed.

He was lifted into the open air. Little Horse saw a sight that took his breath.

Horses! But such horses! They were bigger than the animal who carried him. Taller than the hills of his valley. Some of the horses

ran free. Others were in a strange wooden cave.

The animal who held him turned. Little Horse could no longer see the land of big horses. He struggled for one last look, but he was carried away.

When they stopped, Little Horse looked around with wide eyes. The sun, the clouds, the sky were gone. Where was he?

Another animal was there—smaller. The sounds this animal made were softer.

Little Horse felt himself being given to this smaller, softer animal. The animal held him gently, shielding him the way his mother curled her body around him when he slept.

His ears twitched to hear the sounds of the big horses. Little Horse could hear them, but the neighs were distant. The sounds were almost like the ones he heard in the valley when the horses played in the upper meadow.

Little Horse at Home

Later that day, Little Horse was set down in front of a wooden cave. It looked just like the one he had seen earlier, in the land of the big horses.

The cave was in the open air, and Little Horse could see the big horses in the distance. The horses were no longer in the field but were resting in their cave.

Little Horse sensed this was his new home, and he went inside.

When he looked around he saw there were oats to eat, and there was water to drink. There was even a bed of soft grass.

Little Horse turned around twice, then lay down, curled up in the soft nest.

The smaller animal watched through his doorway. He made soft, gentle sounds.

Night came. Little Horse saw the stars. He saw the moon. It was the same moon, the same stars of his homeland.

Little Horse thought that someday . . . someday when he was as wise as his mother and as strong as his father . . . he might set out for home.

He knew the way. First he would cross the land of the big horses. Then he would head away from the rising sun until he heard the rippling water of the stream.

He would hide in a cave until night.

Then, with the stars and the moon to guide him, he would follow the stream to his valley.

Little Horse fell asleep dreaming of the journey.

About the Author

Betsy Byars is the author of many award-winning and popular books for children, including the Golly Sisters series, illustrated by Sue Truesdell, and *My Dog, My Hero*, written with her daughters, Betsy Duffey and Laurie Myers, and illustrated by Loren Long. Ms. Byars was awarded the Newbery Medal for her novel *The Summer of the Swans*. She and her husband live in South Carolina.

About the Illustrator

David McPhail is the highly acclaimed author and illustrator of a number of books for children, including *Mole Music*, *The Teddy Bear*, and the popular Pig Pig stories. He lives with his family in Portsmouth, New Hampshire.

Here is another
Early Chapter Book
you will enjoy:

Little Raccoon

by master storyteller **Lilian Moore**
illustrated by **Doug Cushman**